AFTERSHOCK !

For Megan – who's been very patient!

ORCHARD BOOKS
96 Leonard Street, London EC2A 4XD
Orchard Books Australia
14 Mars Road, Lane Cove, NSW 2066
First published in Great Britain in 2000
First paperback publication 2001
Text © Tony Bradman 2000
Inside Illustrations © David Kearney 2000
The right of Tony Bradman to be identified as the author
and David Kearney as the illustrator of this work has been asserted by them
in accordance with the Copyright, Designs and Patents Act, 1988.
A CIP catalogue record for this book is available
from the British Library.
1 86039 830 8 (hb)
1 84121 552 X (pb)
1 3 5 7 9 10 8 6 4 2 (hb)
1 3 5 7 9 10 8 6 4 2 (pb)
Printed in Great Britain

TONY BRADMAN

AFTERSHOCK!

 ORCHARD BOOKS

One

Jodie sat silently in the back seat of the
rental car and sulkily watched the California
scenery rolling by. The car swept past steep,
wooded hills and went through a small town,
coming eventually to a rickety bridge that
took them over a tumbling, rock-filled river.
Jodie glanced down, unimpressed.

'Not far now, kids!' said Dad from the front passenger seat in that awful Aren't-We-Having-Such-A-Great-Time? tone of voice Jodie loathed. She was sitting behind him, and he turned to give her a grin. But Jodie didn't respond, his smile faded, and he turned round again, his neck reddening.

'That must be the cabin up ahead,' said Melissa, who was driving. A moment later they slowed, eased on to a patch of rough grass, then came to a halt. Before them in the late afternoon sunlight stood a small wooden house with lots of peeling paintwork. There were no other houses anywhere nearby.

'Hey, where are we?' asked Matt, Melissa's son, who was sitting next to Jodie, behind his mum. Matt turned off his Walkman, pulled out the ear-pieces, peered through the window. 'Why have we stopped?'

'Because we've arrived at our fabulous, luxury vacation shack in the mountains, dummy,' said Jodie, witheringly. 'I can't wait to see inside.'

'Don't start, Jodie,' said Dad, quietly, frowning at her. 'Please?'

'Come on, Matt,' said Melissa quickly, opening her door. 'According to the agent in San Francisco, the key should be under that big pot on the porch. You and Jodie will be OK with the bags, won't you, John?'

'No problem,' said Dad, pressing the button that popped the trunk.

Dad got out, and so did Jodie and Matt. Melissa was already heading for the cabin, and Matt followed behind. Jodie watched them go, the tall, dark-haired woman and the boy who looked like her. Then Jodie

slouched to the trunk, hands in the side
pockets of her combats. Dad lifted the lid.
But he didn't reach in for the luggage. He
faced Jodie instead, and the two of them
stared at each other for a second. Jodie's dad
was taller than Melissa, but skinny, with blue
eyes and the kind of fair hair that always
seemed to flop into them. Jodie was small
and dark, more like her mum.

'Right, so what's it going
to be?' Dad said firmly,

giving Jodie a stern look. 'Some peace and quiet to end the trip on a positive note, or more bad behaviour? I warn you, Jodie, my patience is wearing perilously thin.'

'Bad behaviour?' spluttered Jodie, trying her best to sound totally innocent, although she knew exactly what she'd been doing. She even felt a twinge of guilt, but refused to give in to it. 'Me? I can't think what you mean,' she said.

'Really?' said Dad. 'Well, *I* can't believe you're the same lovely, sweet Jodie I used to know. You've argued and sulked and been horrible since the day we left home. In fact, you've nearly wrecked the entire holiday.'

'Good,' snapped Jodie. There was obviously no point in keeping up a pretence any more. 'I didn't want to be dragged along on this stupid trip in the first place,' she added. 'But then nobody cares what *I* want, do they?'

'That's not true,' said Dad quietly, and sighed. 'Listen, Jodie, I realise it's been pretty tough for you since your mother and I separated. It hasn't been much of a picnic for me, either, not until I met Melissa, at least...'

Jodie stood there tight-lipped while Dad droned on. She had heard it all plenty of times during the last few years. Her parents had grown apart, it wasn't actually anybody's fault, they both still loved her, of course *she* was the important one... None of it was any help, however, mostly because Jodie didn't want to accept what had happened. She wished her parents hadn't split up, and that things were the same as they'd been before.

But that wasn't what her mum and dad were hoping to hear, especially now they were both busily building new lives for themselves. Jodie lived with her dad in their old house and stayed with her mum at the weekends. Mum had a boyfriend, and Dad had met Melissa about six months ago.

Then Dad had announced that Melissa and Matt would be moving in. He had also said the four of them would be taking 'a terrific trip to California' together so they could 'all get to know each other'. And he'd seemed surprised that Jodie had absolutely hated both ideas from the beginning.

But he just didn't understand how she *felt*. If only somebody did, Jodie thought. She had no brothers or sisters, no special friend she could talk to about her feelings, so she simply had to keep everything bottled up – except when she argued or sulked or was horrible. Not that any of it came naturally to her. Dad was right, she'd always been sweet-tempered until the separation, and she'd had to work quite hard at being difficult.

She'd definitely got the hang of it over the last two weeks, though.

'Earth calling Dad,' said Jodie at last, interrupting him in full flow. Dad paused and looked at her, a puzzled expression on his face. 'Have you nearly finished?' asked Jodie. 'Or will we be spending the night out here?'

For a second, Jodie wondered whether she might have pushed her luck. Dad seemed on the verge of losing his temper with her. But finally he took a deep breath instead, reached into the trunk, and started pulling out the luggage.

'Just make an effort, will you, Jodie?' he said. 'For all our sakes.'

'Huh!' snorted Jodie. She picked up her bag and headed for the cabin.

As she reached the porch, she noticed a flash of movement in a stand of trees nearby. She looked round and saw a pair of chipmunks and a couple of squirrels, the four little creatures scampering away from the cabin. Then there was a sound of wild thrashing and fluttering, and suddenly two small birds burst out of one of the trees and darted into the sky, squawking loudly, leaves and twigs falling to the ground as they sped away too.

It seemed odd somehow, Jodie thought, the hairs on the back of her neck rising, even scary, like something in a movie designed to unsettle you. Then she tutted and shook her head, cross with herself for getting spooked so easily. What it really meant was that this place was so boring even the local wildlife had gone totally nuts and finally decided to escape.

Jodie barged into the cabin and let the door slam shut behind her.

TWO

Jodie dropped her bag on the floor and surveyed the interior of the cabin. It was bigger inside than she'd thought it would be. The room in front of her contained a large couch, a couple of armchairs, a TV. To her left was a kitchen area. Jodie could see a big fridge and a long counter with a phone on the wall above it. There were two sliding glass doors in the cabin's rear wall. They were open, and Jodie glimpsed Matt on the deck outside.

There were three doors to her right, and Melissa appeared through the furthest one. She stopped when she saw Jodie, and smiled nervously.

'It's not bad, is it?' said Melissa. 'That's the bathroom,' she added, nodding at the middle door. 'Your dad and I can sleep in here,' she said, pointing behind her, 'and if you like, you can have the room at the front.'

'Er...*hello*?' said Jodie, giving Melissa her special Wow-You-Must-Be-*So*-Stupid look. 'Aren't you forgetting somebody? I mean, there is absolutely no *way* I'm sharing a room with Matt. And that's final.'

'You don't have to,' said Matt cheerfully

as he stepped in from the deck. He sat on the couch cross-legged and picked up the TV remote. 'I'm taking the couch. You should check out the view, Jodie. It's terrific.'

'No thanks,' snapped Jodie, automatically resisting any attempt by Matt to be friendly. 'I've seen enough views on this trip to last me a lifetime.'

And with that, she picked up her bag and stomped off to her room.

But Jodie sneaked on to the deck later, while Dad and Melissa were busy unpacking in their room, and Matt was fetching his Walkman from the car. He was wrong, though. The view wasn't terrific. It was *awesome*.

Behind the cabin was a deep canyon, the deck sticking out over a rocky slope that fell steeply to dark woods below. The

opposite slope rose in the distance, and above it all was the clear blue sky of a California afternoon. Jodie stood with the warmth of the sun on her face, thinking about that conversation with her dad, and found herself weakening. She was tired of being resentful and miserable. All she really wanted was to be happy...

Then she heard Melissa and Dad talking and laughing inside their room – the window to the deck was slightly open – and Jodie's heart hardened once more. She turned on her heel and went back inside, just as Matt came through the front door. He flopped on the couch, dumped his Walkman beside him, and started zapping through TV channels with the remote.

Dad and Melissa emerged from their room again soon after.

'Hey, you two,' said Dad brightly. 'How about driving into town for a look around? We could find somewhere to get a burger, if you like.'

'You can count me out,' said Jodie. 'I thought it seemed like a real dump. And I don't want a burger. I've decided I'm going vegetarian.'

Dad gazed unbelievingly at her for a second... and then his shoulders slumped. Melissa glanced at him, and gave his arm a gentle squeeze.

'We can't leave you here all on your own, Jodie,' Dad said at last.

'Don't worry, I'll stay,' said Matt, without shifting his attention from the screen. 'I don't think I've seen this episode of *The Simpsons* before.'

'That's very nice of you, Matt,' said Dad, 'but I don't know...'

'Oh, relax, John,' said Melissa. 'We won't be long, and we can bring them a take-out. I'm sure we can find you something meat-free, Jodie. I think it's a very good thing you're going vegetarian. I wish I could do it.'

Jodie flashed Melissa a sickly sweet, totally insincere smile.

'OK,' sighed Dad, defeated. 'We'll see you in a little while.'

Dad and Melissa left, and Jodie went over to the window. She watched them get into the car and drive towards the bridge in the distance. Then she headed for the kitchen area. She felt thirsty, and wanted a drink.

There was nothing in the fridge, so it would just have to be water, she realised.

Jodie found a cupboard that contained a pile of plates and some glasses. She filled a glass at the sink, then headed off to her room.

She walked past Matt on the way. He looked at her and seemed to be about to speak, but Jodie sniffed and ignored him. He probably wanted her to thank him for rescuing her from going into town, she thought. Well, he was out of luck. Jodie had to admit it had been a kind thing to do, but she wasn't ready to get that chummy with him yet. So she slammed her door, put the glass of water on the low cabinet beside the bed, and lay down.

Her room was larger than the other bedroom, with a bigger wardrobe and an armchair in the corner. And she had it all to herself, she thought with satisfaction... She sat up to get a book from her bag and take a sip from her drink. At last she had some peace, a moment to herself.

Jodie reached for the glass beside her, but before she picked it up, she stopped. She suddenly felt spooked again, the same as she had done when she'd seen those animals and birds outside. It was very quiet. Eerily so.

That's very strange, she thought, looking at the glass. The surface of the water in it seemed to be trembling, and the sight

reminded her of a scene
in a movie, she realised – that bit in
Jurassic Park where the puddle shakes
ominously when the T-Rex is coming. Jodie
sat watching it, fascinated. Now the water
wasn't simply trembling any more, it was
starting to slop over the sides of the glass,
and the glass was beginning to dance across
the top of the cabinet. And that was because
the cabinet itself was shaking.

Then Jodie realised the bed she was sitting on was shaking too, and jolting up and down. Suddenly there was an almighty crash in the room beyond, and Matt cried out, sounding very scared. The shaking and jolting was getting worse, and worse, and worse, and raw fear raced through Jodie's veins. She leapt to her feet... and couldn't believe what she felt.

The *floor* was moving! The walls were shuddering as well – and then the window shattered. Big shards of glass flew across the room, Jodie ducked instinctively, the floor tipped, she lost her balance, and fell headlong.

She tried to stand but the floor was bucking and heaving beneath her feet. Then Jodie looked up, and saw the wardrobe toppling towards her...

Three

Jodie screamed and turned away, covering the back of her head with her hands, waiting for the impact, terrified of the pain she thought she was about to feel. The front of the wardrobe whacked into her, knocking her flat, but it didn't crush her, and Jodie realised she had been saved by the bed. The

upper half of the wardrobe had hit it, leaving her squashed in the small space between its lower half and the bedroom's heaving floor.

Not that she had time to feel relieved. Panic surged through her as she lay there. What was going on? Jodie had never experienced anything like this in her life before, so she had no idea what to do. She only knew one thing – she wasn't going to stay where she was. She pulled herself out, jumped to her feet, grabbed the door handle. It wouldn't budge at first, but she yanked and yanked, finally managing to pull the door open.

Beyond it was a scene from a nightmare. The cabin was rocking, the walls seemed to be rippling as they went in and out, the floor was bucking and jumping, plates and glasses were leaping from the kitchen cupboards and hitting the floor with *SMASH!* after *SMASH!*, the air was filled with dust and the sound of wood snapping and metal squealing and a deep rumbling, and the TV was on its front with smoke pouring from it.

And Matt was nowhere to be seen, either.

He had been sitting on the couch a moment ago, but now it was empty. It was also juddering towards the rear doors, both of which suddenly cracked from top to bottom just as if they'd been bashed by somebody invisible, splinters of glass falling to the floor both inside and outside. Jodie flinched, her mind reeling, and desperately gripped the door-frame.

But that only made her feel worse. A terrible shaking passed up her arms and into her shoulders. It grew stronger, and stronger, and stronger, and just when Jodie thought she couldn't stand it for a second more... it stopped. It was as if it had been switched off, and silence descended.

A last plate slipped free – and the *CRASH!* as it hit the floor instantly brought Jodie back to her senses. She released her hold on the door-frame and advanced slowly into the room, one very careful step after another, testing the floor in front of her as if it might give way at any second.

'Matt?' she said, her voice unsteady but sounding strangely loud, her heart thumping like mad against her ribs. Jodie wanted to find Matt, but she was frightened. What if he'd been crushed as she almost had been, and was lying somewhere bleeding... and dead? 'Matt, where are you?'

'I'm here,' said Matt's voice, but Jodie couldn't see him. Then his head appeared from behind an armchair, and relief flooded through her. Matt crawled out on his hands and knees, stood up, and dusted himself down. Jodie almost wanted to hug him... but she didn't. 'Are you OK?' he said.

'Yeah, I suppose so,' Jodie replied, getting her voice under control, trying to sound cool and superior and totally unafraid. Her heart was still pounding like crazy, but she wasn't about to let Matt think she was rattled. 'Except for a sudden allergy to large falling wardrobes, that is,' she said.

'I'm sorry?' said Matt, sounding puzzled. 'Oh, I get it,' he said with a weak smile. 'I know what you mean. I don't like TV sets that try to leap into my lap, either. Even if they are showing *The Simpsons* at the time.'

'I take it we've just survived an earthquake,' said Jodie, gingerly heading for the kitchen area and peering over the counter. A heap of smashed crockery covered the floor. 'Whoa, plate graveyard!' she said.

'Yeah, that was *definitely* a quake,' said Matt distractedly, his gaze roaming round the

walls. He almost seemed to be studying them, Jodie thought. 'A big one, too. The shaking must have lasted nearly a minute.'

'I can't say I was timing it,' Jodie muttered. 'And would you mind not staring at the walls like that? You're making me feel uncomfortable.'

'Don't they seem a bit odd to you?' said Matt. 'I mean, they're not as straight as

they should be. It's as if the cabin's sort of...
leaning now.'

Jodie looked, and thought he might
be right. The walls did appear to be tilted
slightly. But then she remembered
who she was talking to, and
started to feel annoyed.
How could Melissa's son
be right about anything?
'I don't think so,'
said Jodie firmly.
'It's probably
just you.

Maybe you should ask your mother if you can have your eyesight tested.'

'Listen,' said Matt seriously, walking towards her. He peered over the counter at the smashed plates. 'Sometimes after a big quake, there are...'

'Wait a second,' Jodie interrupted. 'What makes you such an expert all of a sudden? Forgive me, but I don't remember anybody telling me that you were a professor in... in earthquake-ology, or whatever it's called.'

'It's seismology,' said Matt, frowning. 'And I'm not an expert. I've just read a few books and surfed a few websites. I got interested when Mum said we were coming to California. They have a lot of quakes here.'

'Hey, I know that!' said Jodie, her irritation deepening. 'It's because of the San Andreas Fault. We learned about it in geography last year, so there. Still, somebody might have told us they were expecting this one.'

'They couldn't have done,' said Matt. 'It's impossible to predict when an earthquake will happen. Although there's a theory that sometimes just before a quake the local wildlife gets spooked and acts a little strangely.'

'You can say that again,' said Jodie, thinking of what she'd seen earlier. Spooked was the right way to describe how those animals and birds had behaved. Matt raised an eyebrow, but Jodie didn't elaborate. 'Anyway, I wonder whether my dad and your mum got caught in it?' she said.

'No idea,' said Matt. 'It depends how badly it hit the town, I guess.'

Matt paused... and they stared at each

other while they both thought. Then they
hurried to the cabin's front windows. Jodie
was amazed to see a giant zigzag crack
across the patch of grass outside.
Then she raised her eyes,
followed the curve of the road
downhill, and gasped in
surprise.

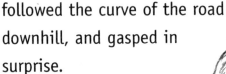

   The bridge over the
river had completely
collapsed.

Four

Jodie looked anxiously at the scene below them. She could just make out a scattering of girders and planks dangling on the torn-off road edge, and more on the rocks of the opposite bank. The river was racing, and she guessed the rest of the bridge must have been swept away in the torrent. She just hoped no one had been on the bridge when it had gone...

The town was no more than a kilometre away, so it should have been clearly visible from the cabin. But a column of thick black smoke had appeared from somewhere beyond the river, and was already drifting down and spreading, covering the town's buildings in an impenetrable haze.

As Jodie and Matt watched, the smoke started creeping across the river, like some kind of giant evil monster determined to eat everything in its path. It began to envelop a line of cars that had stopped in the road on the other side of the bridge, and the people standing there who had got out of them.

Jodie could hear sirens wailing faintly. She shivered, and realised she felt cold even though the sun was shining warmly through the window. The world had changed with terrifying speed, and she didn't like it at all.

'That's them down there,' she said, quietly. 'I'm sure it is.'

'It isn't,' said Matt. 'None of those cars are the right colour.'

'How do you know?' snapped Jodie. 'The smoke is too thick. And where's *that* coming from? Don't tell me there's a volcano here too.'

'It's probably a fire,' said Matt. 'They often happen after earthquakes in towns and cities. They can be caused by damaged power cables, or...'

'Just cut to the chase, Einstein,' said Jodie fiercely, turning to look at him. Matt took a step backwards and frowned at her. 'Do you think my dad and your mum made it across the bridge before it collapsed?' she said.

'They might have,' said Matt, cautiously, biting his lip. He looked out of the window again. 'But the only way to be really certain is to go and see,' he said. 'Besides, I don't think we should stay in here any longer.'

'What are you talking about now?' said Jodie.

'I was trying to tell you,' said Matt. 'This cabin might not be safe...'

She listened impatiently as Matt explained what he meant. He told her that all the information he'd read on earthquakes had said remaining inside damaged buildings after a tremor could be very dangerous. It seemed the quake might not actually be over, and that there might be something called aftershocks, tremors following the main one, smaller but still dangerous.

Jodie could feel herself gradually being

persuaded. In any case, part of her was desperate to find her dad. But there was another part of her that simply wanted to sit tight, stay right where she was, bury her head deep in the sand until the trouble had gone. Then maybe she would look up and discover the world had returned to normal, to how *she* wanted it to be. A silent, intense struggle went on inside her as Matt talked – and as usual, it was the burying-her-head-in-the-sand part that won.

'You're asking me to believe it's safer outside than it is in here?' Jodie exploded at last. Matt paused, and took another step backwards. 'With cracks in the ground, collapsing bridges, damaged power cables, fires?' said Jodie, advancing and jabbing him in the chest. 'A likely story, buster.'

'Come on, Jodie,' said Matt at last, grabbing the finger she'd been using to jab him.

Jodie wrenched it free of his grip and glared at him.

'We've got to go outside,' Matt said, turning towards the door. 'You're being stupid.'

'How dare you call me stupid!' Jodie yelled. 'That's it, I've had enough. If *you* say the best thing to do is leave the cabin, then I reckon it's bound to get me killed. Read my

lips, dummy. I'm not going anywhere.'

'Oh, that's terrific,' said Matt sarcastically, turning back to her. 'So you want to get us both killed instead. Look, I know you don't like me, but...'

'Excuse me?' said Jodie. 'Nobody's ordering *you* to stay. I'll be fine on my own. To be honest, I'd appreciate some privacy. After two weeks of being driven round California with you and your mother I deserve it.'

'But what about your dad?' asked Matt.
Jodie was pleased to see her goading was
having an effect. Matt was starting to
develop an angry scowl himself. 'Don't you
even want to find out if he's all right?' he
asked.

'Of course I do,' said Jodie. She walked
back to the counter, then turned to face Matt.
'I just think there's got to be an easier way.
Such as asking the local police, for instance.
They'll know what's going on.'

Jodie picked up the receiver to call 911,
the emergency number. She'd seen it done
often enough on TV and in the movies, and
it always worked there. But it didn't work for
her. The phone was stone dead.

And it stayed dead, however hard she
jabbed at the buttons.

'Now you know why I didn't bother to try

it,' said Matt, folding his arms. 'The first thing that goes in an earthquake is the phone system, especially in an area like this. I'll bet most of the lines are down.'

'What about a mobile?' said Jodie. 'Dad always has his with him.'

'I haven't brought mine,' said Matt. 'And didn't I hear your dad say he'd confiscated yours a while back because of your bad behaviour?'

'Listen, smarty-pants,' said Jodie angrily. 'I'm sick and tired of your...'

'Shush!' said Matt, suddenly. 'Did you feel that?'

'What?' said Jodie, nervously. She stood very still.

'I'm sure it was a tremor, an aftershock,' said Matt.

Jodie noticed he was whispering, almost

as if he thought speaking loudly might make the ground start shaking once more.

'There might be another any second...' he added, and began moving carefully towards the cabin's front door.

'You must have imagined it,' said Jodie, hardly daring to breathe.

'I didn't,' Matt replied, fear in his voice. 'Here it comes again!'

Jodie heard a soft tinkling from beyond the counter. She glanced over, and saw that the heap of broken crockery was trembling. As she watched, the pile shifted. Then there was a terrible, ear-splitting, splintering noise...

And the floor beneath her feet suddenly seemed to disappear.

Five

For a second Jodie thought she must have plunged through a trapdoor she hadn't spotted till then, although she knew that was crazy. Then she fell heavily on her front, banging her face on the floor, and she realised with a shock that the cabin had suddenly and terrifyingly tipped backwards...

and was moving, that ear-splitting, splintering noise getting louder and louder.

Jodie started to slide feet first down the smooth, polished floorboards, desperately scrabbling for a hold. But she only slid faster and faster, panicking, until somehow she sensed the bottom of the counter beside her, and managed to turn on her side and grab the metal support at the end. She stopped abruptly, gasping as her arm nearly popped out of its socket, and quickly swung her other arm

round so she could use that hand too.

Jodie hung on with both hands. She felt the heap of broken crockery stream past her legs, she heard everything still in the cupboards fly out at once, and she yelled in pain as several large pots and pans bounced off her. The floor was juddering, and there were cracking, tearing noises, and a rumbling so deep it made her teeth hurt. Jodie looked round and saw the front door wide open, and Matt desperately holding on to the doorstep.

Then her attention was caught by one of the armchairs...which was starting to move too. She watched in horror as it accelerated towards the sliding doors and hit them with a *CRASH!* that shattered the cracked glass. The other armchair followed the same path, as did the TV, the couch,and anything else in the room that wasn't attached. Soon there was a huge log-jam of furniture and smashed objects covering most of the rear wall.

That seemed to push the back of the cabin even lower, and it tilted at an alarming angle. Another movie image briefly flashed into Jodie's mind, this time those terrible last scenes of

Titanic when the great ship tilts ever higher in the water and everything slides down its decks, people, objects, everything.

Then the cabin suddenly slowed and paused, teetering...

Jodie could hear the high-pitched grinding of metal under enormous strain, a sound that was worse than fingernails scraped down a blackboard – and then the sliding doors burst from their frames. Most of the furniture instantly shot out and vanished, taking the deck railing with it. At the same moment, the rear of the cabin rose sharply, and Jodie nearly lost her grip.

She closed her eyes and clung on as tightly as she could to the support, and concentrated her whole being on *not* letting go... and then after a while she realised the cabin wasn't moving any more. The juddering and the splintering and the rumbling had ceased too, and all she could hear now was a gentle, ominous creaking, and the wind whistling softly outside.

'Whoa, talk about extreme...' whispered Jodie after a few seconds of peace. She opened her eyes, but didn't relax her grip on the support. If anything, she held on even more tightly than before, and pulled herself up a little further. She realised she was breathing heavily, and one side of her face seemed to be wet. 'I don't believe that just happened,' she said.

'Well, it did,' Matt snapped, real anger in his voice. Jodie looked up at him, surprised. He was still hanging on to the doorstep, which was several metres *above* her now, the sight making her feel sick. 'I *told* you it wasn't safe to stay in here,' he continued, glaring at her. 'But you wouldn't listen, would you? And I'll bet you don't have a clue what caused it, either.'

'Well, you couldn't be more wrong, Mr

Boring-Nerdy-Know-It-All,' Jodie snapped. 'I'd say the ground beneath the back of the cabin gave way because of the aftershock, or whatever it was. Am I right, or am I right?'

'Top marks,' said Matt, taking a glance over his shoulder. 'But that crack outside is a heck of a lot wider, too. If you ask me, this particular part of California is getting ready to slip to the bottom of the canyon.'

Jodie turned cautiously to look at the hole in the cabin's rear wall where the sliding doors had once been. Through it she could see the battered deck beyond, and the steep, rocky, downward slope to the dark woods... which were easily more than two hundred metres below.

Jodie imagined the cabin breaking free, and the wild ride that would be bound to follow. She gulped, and felt panic rising inside her again. There wouldn't be much left of the cabin, she thought. Or them, for that matter.

'OK, you've totally convinced me,' she said, pulling up her legs and pushing herself off the floor. 'You're a genius...and I'm out of here.'

'No, wait!' yelled Matt. 'Stay where you are! *Don't move yet!*'

'Hey, what is it with you?' Jodie asked, 'First you give me a hard time because I won't leave,' she said, getting to her feet, 'then when I...'

The cabin shifted slightly, and Jodie froze, her stomach churning. A last piece of broken crockery tinkled past her foot, skittered towards the hole, bounced on to the deck, and flew into space – but the cabin didn't follow. Jodie quickly lowered herself to the floor and gripped the support till her hands hurt. She buried her face deep in her arms, and felt her heart hammering in her chest. She was trembling, her eyes filled with tears...and she knew that no matter how miserable she'd been, she didn't want to die. and she also knew that death might only be seconds away.

'Listen, Jodie,' she heard Matt urgently whispering above her. 'We'll have to be very careful, OK? I've got a feeling that any sudden movement could set it off again. But I think I can see a way for us to make it to firm ground, although you'll have to get to me...slowly. Here, take my hand.'

Jodie raised her head and looked up at him. Matt was holding on to the doorstep with one arm, and reaching out with the other, an encouraging expression on his face.

His hand was less than a metre away from her.

'You have *got* to be joking,' she said, her voice quivering.

'Don't be afraid, Jodie,' said Matt, stretching further towards her. 'You can make it...so long as you don't make any sharp movements, that is.'

'I'm not afraid,' Jodie snapped. 'I just don't need *your* help, dummy.'

Matt snatched his hand back as if it had been scalded.

Six

'I don't believe this, I really don't,' Matt
muttered, practically spitting the words out,
his face dark with fury, his eyes narrowed.
'Here I am doing my best to save your life,
and all you can do is call me names,' he said.
'For Christ's sake, we wouldn't *be* in this
situation if it wasn't for you.'

'Hey, that's not fair,' murmured Jodie, sure she could feel the floor moving beneath her. 'You can't blame me for the earthquake...'

'But then I suppose it's what I should have expected from somebody as selfish as you,' Matt continued, ignoring what she'd just said, swept along on the tide of his rant. 'Somebody who's done nothing but moan and whine and throw tantrums every single day for the last two weeks.'

'Now just you wait a minute,' said Jodie, wanting to defend herself, but daunted by his anger. 'There was at least one day when I...'

'Everybody's bent over backwards to keep you happy,' Matt said, finally locking his gaze on to her eyes. 'Your dad and my mum couldn't have tried harder,' he said, 'and I've been as friendly as I know how. But is that good enough for Little Miss Moody? Oh no, obviously not.'

Jodie tried to look as if she didn't give a hoot about what he was saying, but it wasn't long before she began to find it impossible to maintain her usual snooty expression. That slight twinge of guilt had made a definite comeback, and it made a potent mix with the fear she was feeling.

'OK, OK,' she muttered eventually. 'So I won't win the Most-Popular-Person-On-Vacation Award this year. I don't think I'll be losing much sleep over it, actually. I didn't want to come on this stupid trip anyway.'

'Well, that makes two of us,' Matt said bitterly. 'But then I never wanted my mum and dad to get divorced in the first place, and I certainly didn't much like the idea of coming to live with a couple of people I don't know from Adam. Not that anybody seems interested in what *I* feel.'

Matt looked away from her and fell into silence, while Jodie let his words sink in. She'd been thinking much the same herself recently, so maybe she had a lot more in common with Matt than she'd realised. It simply hadn't occurred to her he might have exactly the same kind of feelings and worries that she did. He'd just been Matt, Melissa's son, the geeky moron who sat next to her in the rental car, the dummy who had been nice to *her* however mean she had been to *him*, she thought.

Jodie was still gripping the support tightly with both hands, and they were hurting badly now. She could hear the wind whistling outside, and the cabin creaking around her. And she could feel her cheeks flushing with shame at the thought of what she'd been like over the last two weeks.

How could she have let herself become so horrible? Whatever she felt about her mum and dad separating and Melissa and Dad getting together, Matt hadn't done anything to deserve the treatment she'd given him. He must really hate her guts, Jodie thought, and with good reason, too.

Jodie felt something liquid trickle down her face to the corner of her mouth, and licked at it instinctively. The taste told her immediately she was bleeding, and she realised the stiffness above her eyebrow must mean she'd cut her forehead when she'd fallen. Her arms and shoulders were beginning to ache, and she didn't know how much longer she could hold on. But unless Matt helped her, there was nothing else she could do.

'OK, Matt,' she said at last, shivering with the fear that still filled her. She wanted to get out of there *so* badly... 'I admit it. You're right.'

'About what?' he snapped, turning to look at her again.

'More or less everything, I suppose,' she muttered gloomily. She could see the dust and dirt and fear on Matt's face, and she lowered her eyes, unable to meet his fierce stare. 'I should just be grateful that you're even willing to help me,' she said, 'especially as I haven't been very friendly to you.'

'Huh,' snorted Matt, carefully pulling himself a little further on to the doorstep. 'That's putting it mildly. And I'm not sure I *do* want to help you. You're only being nice now because you've realised what a mess we're in. The minute we get out you'll probably be just as mean to me as ever.'

'OK, Matt,' said Jodie quietly. She could feel tears in her eyes once more, and suddenly she didn't want to argue with him. It was all too much. 'You save yourself,' she said, 'don't worry about me. I'm pretty certain everybody will be a lot happier and a lot better off if I'm not around.'

'Oh great, here we go,' Matt muttered. 'You really love wallowing in self-pity, don't you, Jodie? Look, forget what I said. I'll help you, so long as you promise to keep that big mouth of yours shut until we're safe, OK?'

'What do you mean, *self-pity*?' she said. 'Why, I've never...'

Jodie didn't finish what she wanted to say, for just at that moment there was a loud crack, and the whole cabin suddenly shifted. She could feel it starting to slip very slowly further down the slope, and she gripped the support, waiting for the movement to stop as before. But this time it didn't, and creaking, splintering, grinding, wrenching noises filled the air again. Jodie could feel the terrible momentum beneath her gathering pace...

'Come *on*, Jodie!' yelled Matt, his face drained, a white mask of panic and terror, his eyes wide. 'Quick, take my hand! It's your only chance!'

Jodie looked up. Matt was still holding on to the doorstep with his left arm and straining towards her with the right. She took one hand off the support, gripped even harder with the other, and reached out to him. Their fingertips were a metre apart, half a metre, a quarter, they were almost touching. Jodie ignored the pain in her shoulders and her other arm, she focused on Matt's hand, she started pushing her feet against the floor...

Their hands met. Matt seized her wrist and hauled. Jodie kept pushing with her feet, and her knees now, and then she was crawling, and then she grabbed Matt's T-shirt with her other hand and scrambled over his back and grabbed the doorstep next to him, where she finally came to a halt.

Then suddenly Matt cried out – and he was gone...

Seven

Jodie realised it must have been her added weight as she clambered over Matt that had loosened his grip, and now he was sliding away from her down the polished floor. She lunged desperately after him with her left hand, holding on to the doorstep with her right, catching one sleeve of his T-shirt, grabbing what felt like a tiny bunch of thin material in her fist.

Matt was on his back, and kept sliding until his T-shirt rucked up under his armpits and *his* weight suddenly dragged on Jodie's arm, almost pulling her down with him. Jodie hung on... and watched horrified as the sleeve slowly started to rip away from the rest of the T-shirt. She tried to haul Matt up, but the harder she pulled, the more the tear lengthened.

Matt looked at his sleeve, then at Jodie, their eyes meeting, and he grabbed her arm with both his hands. He clung on to her and pushed with his feet, just as she had done seconds previously, he pulled himself up along her arm, Jodie screaming at him, 'Come on, Matt, come on!', he grabbed her shoulder...and finally, with a kick and a gasp, he made it.

'Thanks, Jodie,' he said breathlessly as the two of them gripped the doorstep side by side. 'I thought I was a goner there for a moment.'

Jodie didn't reply at first. She could feel that the cabin was still moving, and the creaking and grinding noises were louder than ever. She turned her head and looked outside, and was shocked to see that the zigzag crack in the grass had become a deep, dark gash across the ground, the nearest edge definitely moving, small rocks and clods of soil and grass falling off.

The far edge had risen at least a metre, too, and as Jodie watched, it rose a little more, the cabin juddering sickeningly in response. But the cabin's downward momentum felt relentless, unstoppable…and deadly. Jodie thought it couldn't possibly be long before this whole side of the hill slid right to the bottom of the canyon, just as Matt had predicted.

'And I think we'll *both* be goners if we don't get out of here pretty soon,' said Jodie at last. Matt glanced at her, and Jodie tried to smile. 'I know, I should have listened,' she said, gabbling the words, her voice shaking, fear coursing through her veins. 'Well, I'm all ears now, and I hope you've got a plan, because I don't see how we're going to do it.'

Matt switched his attention to the crack, and scanned its length.

'Look, the crack isn't anywhere near as deep over by the trees,' he said, eventually. Jodie followed the direction of his gaze. 'Their roots must be holding the soil together better there. I reckon if we can make it that far, we'll be able to jump across, and then we'll be OK. Er...probably.'

'That's it?' said Jodie, turning to him. 'That's your plan?'

'Yeah,' said Matt with a shrug. 'It is. Got a better one?'

Jodie opened her mouth to speak, but suddenly that ominous rumbling started again, and she felt the cabin's slide starting to pick up speed.

'Actually, no, I haven't,' she said quickly, a wave of sheer terror sweeping through her. 'On the count of three, OK? One...two...*THREE!*'

They scrambled to their feet, linked
hands, and staggered on to the porch. Jodie
felt it shift sharply beneath her as they leapt
to the ground, which started to move even
more quickly. Jodie nearly fell, but Matt
pulled her up, and they ran
over rolling earth and
rocks towards
the crack.

They ran
and they ran,
and Jodie's head was
filled with the sounds of
splintering and grinding and that
awful, deep rumbling, and the crack just
didn't seem to be getting any closer, and
then it was right in front of them, and Jodie
spotted a thick tree root on the other side,
and focused on it.

'Jump, Jodie!' yelled Matt, and that's
what they both did.

Jodie grabbed the root and held on. Matt could only grab loose soil, and slid back, until Jodie shot out her other hand...and caught him. He grabbed her arm, and together they scrabbled against the loose soil, reaching the firmer ground together just as the rumbling became a terrific roar.

They lay on their backs for a second, whimpering, groaning, panting, trying to get their breath back before getting up and staggering further from the dark gash in the earth which had nearly claimed them. Then there was an almighty crescendo of noise, and they turned to look. The cabin had finally come completely adrift, and it shot off down the slope, bumping, banging, bits off the roof flying off, its walls screeching apart as nails and screws gave way, and finally reaching the woods with a mighty...*CRASH!*

'Wow, cool,' said Jodie as silence settled over the canyon. A cloud of dust hung above the woods. 'Now you don't see *that* every day, do you?'

'No, you don't,' said Matt, his eyes focused on the churned-up soil just below where they were standing. Jodie noticed some of it was

still moving slightly. 'Er...I think we might be a little safer elsewhere,' said Matt.

The two of them quickly backed away, then turned and made for the road. They emerged from the trees and stood blinking in the sunlight. Jodie glanced down towards the river and saw a familiar car racing up the hill.

'It's them, I'm sure of it!' said Jodie, a strange mixture of feelings flooding through her – sheer relief that she was safe and Dad was too, guilt at the way she'd been, gratitude to Matt. 'I really *am* sorry about being horrible to you and your mum,' she said, almost choking up, her eyes filling with tears again. 'But after my mum and dad separated, I...'

'Forget it, Jodie,' said Matt quietly, smiling at her. Then he looked away and started brushing himself down. 'You don't have to explain. I know *exactly* how you feel. Maybe we could talk about it some time.'

Jodie smiled back at him. Matt might be the special friend she needed, she realised. They'd helped each other survive an earthquake, hadn't they? So together they could probably handle *anything*.

Even their parents.

The car stopped, and Dad and Melissa jumped out. The town hadn't been that badly damaged, although the roads had been jammed. But they'd managed to cross the river upstream, using a bridge that hadn't collapsed.

'Don't worry, Jodie,' said Dad, his voice shaking, holding her tightly, checking the cut on her forehead. 'Everything's going to be all right.'

And for the first time in ages, Jodie just had to agree...

Why not try these other action-packed stories from Orchard Books?

GHOSTHUNTERS   Anthony Masters

☐	1. Deadly Games	1 86039 815 4	£3.99
☐	2. Haunted School	1 86039 813 8	£3.99
☐	3. Poltergeist	1 86039 814 6	£3.99
☐	4. Possessed	1 86039 816 2	£3.99
☐	5. Dark Tower	1 86039 817 0	£3.99
☐	6. Dancing with the Dead	1 86039 818 9	£3.99

DARK DIARIES   Anthony Masters

☐	1. Dead Ringer	1 86039 943 6	£3.99
☐	2. Fire Starter	1 86039 944 4	£3.99
☐	3. Death Day	1 86039 945 2	£3.99
☐	4. Shock Waves	1 86039 946 0	£3.99

Orchard books are available from all good bookshops,
or can be ordered direct from the publisher:
Orchard Books, PO BOX 29, Douglas IM99 1BQ
Credit card orders please telephone 01624 836000
or fax 01624 837033
or visit our Internet site: www.wattspub.co.uk
or e-mail: bookshop@enterprise.net for details.

To order please quote title, author and ISBN and
your full name and address.
Cheques and postal orders should be made payable to
'Book Post plc.'
Postage and packing is FREE within the UK
(overseas customers should add £1.00 per book).

Prices and availability are subject to change.